Published by Magna Books
Magna Road
Wigston
Leicester LE18 4ZH

Produced by
Twin Books UK Ltd
Kimbolton House
117A Fulham Road
London SW3 6RL

Directed by CND – Muriel Nathan-Deiller
Illustrated by VAn Gool-Lefévre-Loiseaux

ISBN 1 85422 440 9

Printed in Hong Kong

"'VAN GOOL'S'"

Snow White
& the Seven Dwarfs

MAGNA BOOKS

Once upon a time, in a faraway kingdom, there lived seven dwarves who had a wonderful story to tell. People came from near and far to hear how they had once rescued a beautiful Princess. And when they had finished their daily work of mining gold and precious stones, the dwarves would bring out their storybook and recall just how it had happened.

Their story began on a snowy winter's evening many years earlier, as the Queen of their land sat by a window, sewing with finely colored threads.

6

As she sewed, the gentle Queen pricked her finger, and a drop of her blood fell on the snow-covered windowsill. The Queen, who had long been hoping for a child, made a wish. "I wish I had a child with hair as black as night, lips as red as blood, and skin as white as snow," she said.

Later that year, a lovely daughter was born to the Queen, and her wish was fulfilled. The child had night-black hair, red lips, and fair skin. The happy Queen named her child Snow White. But, sadly, the Queen died soon after her daughter was born.

After a time, Snow White's father, the
King, married again.
    The new Queen was also very beautiful,
but she was proud and cold-hearted, unlike
the mother of Snow White.

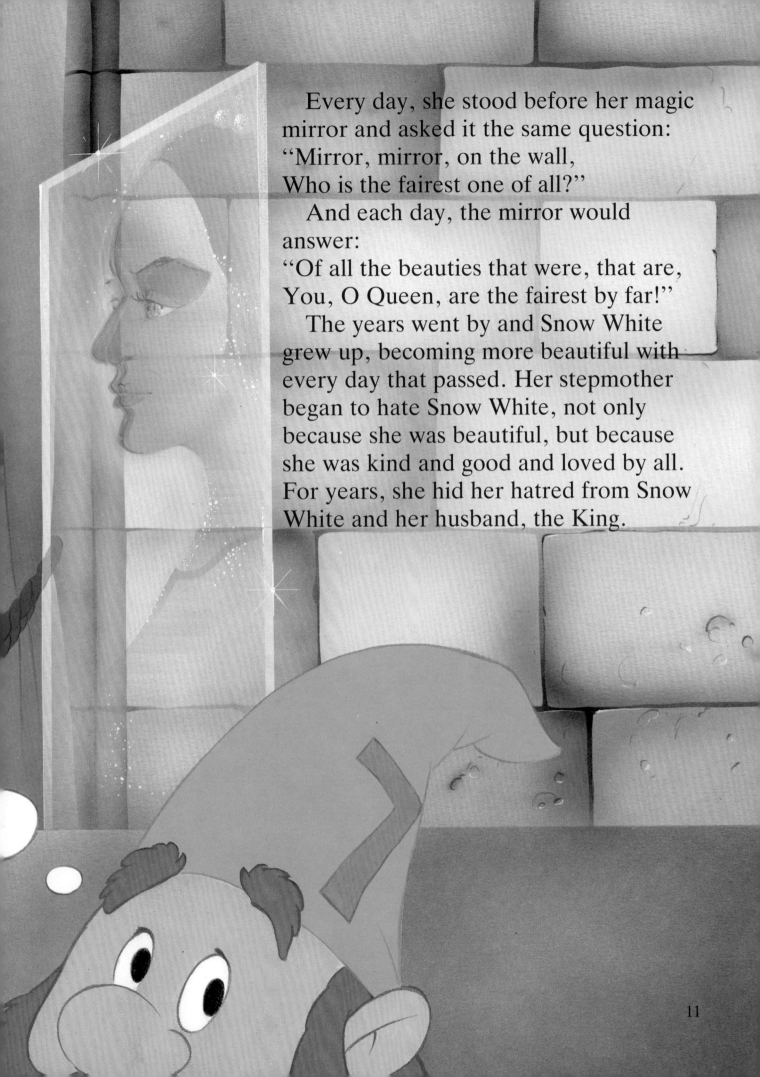

Every day, she stood before her magic mirror and asked it the same question: "Mirror, mirror, on the wall, Who is the fairest one of all?"

And each day, the mirror would answer: "Of all the beauties that were, that are, You, O Queen, are the fairest by far!"

The years went by and Snow White grew up, becoming more beautiful with every day that passed. Her stepmother began to hate Snow White, not only because she was beautiful, but because she was kind and good and loved by all. For years, she hid her hatred from Snow White and her husband, the King.

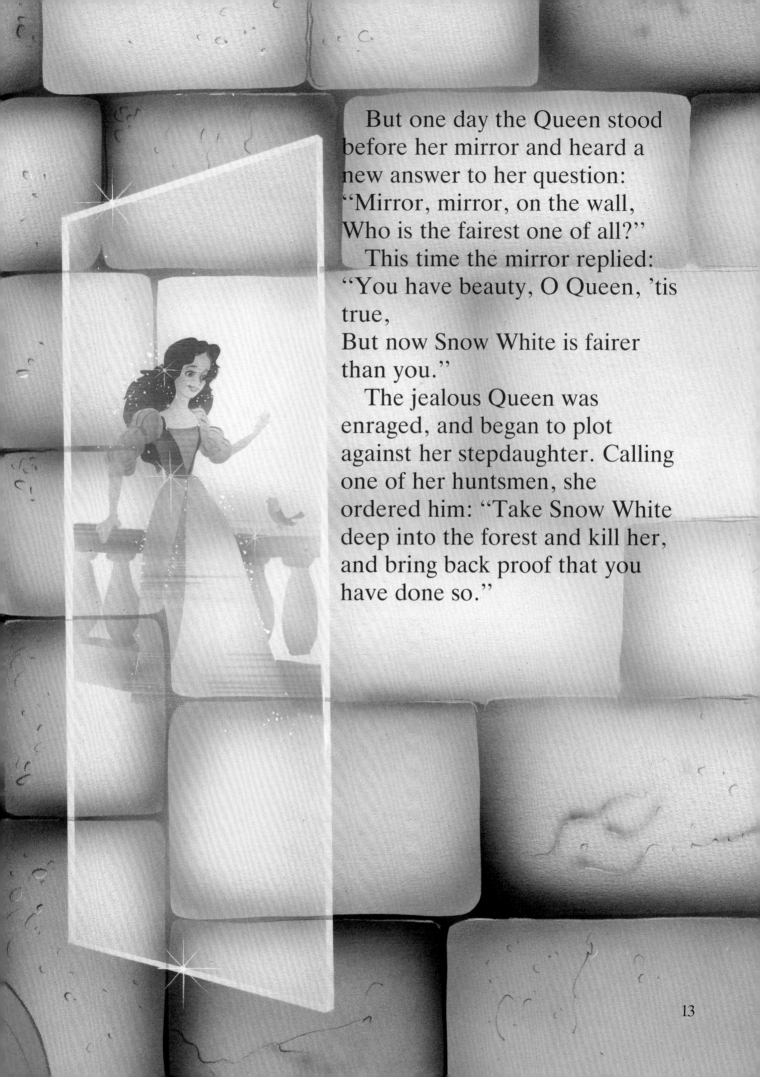

But one day the Queen stood before her mirror and heard a new answer to her question: "Mirror, mirror, on the wall, Who is the fairest one of all?"

This time the mirror replied: "You have beauty, O Queen, 'tis true, But now Snow White is fairer than you."

The jealous Queen was enraged, and began to plot against her stepdaughter. Calling one of her huntsmen, she ordered him: "Take Snow White deep into the forest and kill her, and bring back proof that you have done so."

The huntsman dared not disobey the Queen. Much against his will, he told Snow White that he must go with her next time she visited the forest.

Snow White often walked in the forest, where she could escape from the unkindness of her stepmother and the constant noise and activity of the castle. She enjoyed her quiet hours alone, but she was too kind-hearted to refuse the huntsman's request. Next time she walked in the forest, she allowed him to go with her, as her stepmother had ordered.

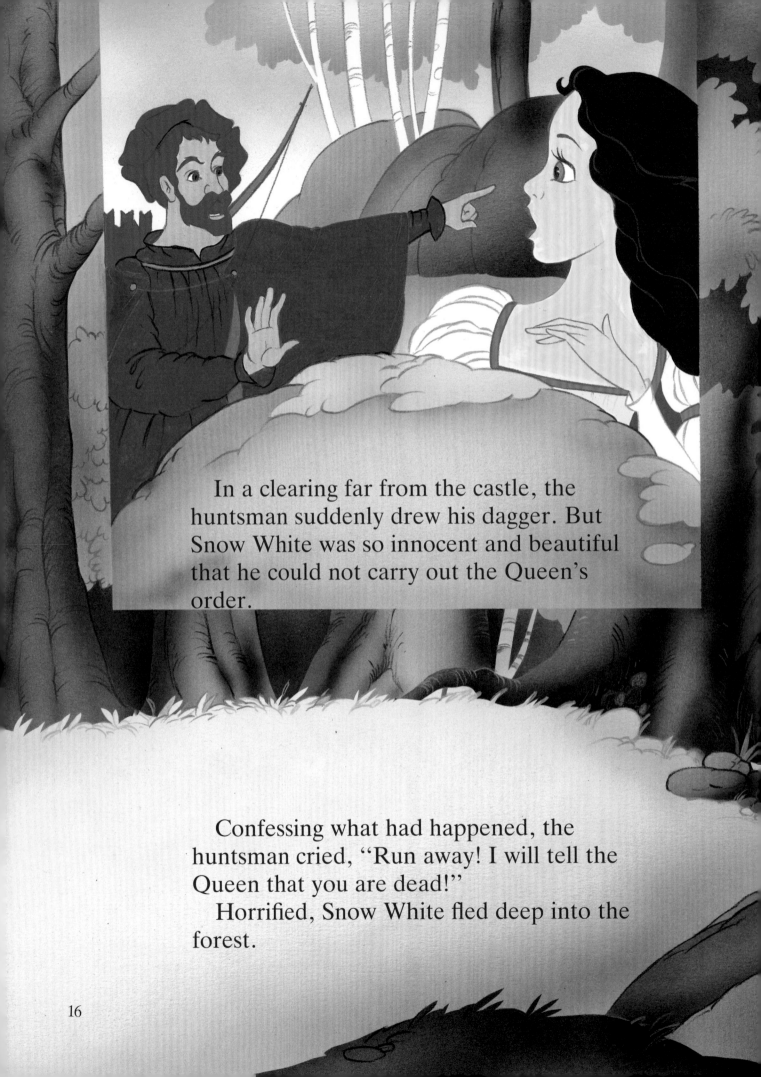

In a clearing far from the castle, the huntsman suddenly drew his dagger. But Snow White was so innocent and beautiful that he could not carry out the Queen's order.

Confessing what had happened, the huntsman cried, "Run away! I will tell the Queen that you are dead!"

Horrified, Snow White fled deep into the forest.

The huntsman killed a young deer and placed its heart in a wooden box. He returned to the castle and presented it to the Queen, saying, "Here is the heart of Snow White, as you commanded."

Snow White had run until she could
go no farther.

Below her she saw a small thatched
cottage nestled in a shady hollow.
"Perhaps I can take shelter there," she
thought. "And get something to eat
before I go on."

From a distance, the small animals of
the forest watched and wondered.

Snow White walked down the hill and
knocked timidly at the door of the cottage.
When there was no answer, she let herself in.

Back at the castle, the Queen asked her magic mirror:
"Mirror, mirror, on the wall, Who's the fairest of them all?"

But the mirror replied:
"Queen, thou art of beauty rare,
But Snow White is a thousand times more fair!"

Then the mirror showed an image of Snow White, entering a little cottage.

"Snow White!" shrieked the enraged Queen. "She lives! The huntsman didn't kill her after all. I shall have to do the job myself."

24

When Snow White entered the cottage, she was surprised to find that everything inside was very small – the cups, the knives and forks, even the beds. The hungry girl poured herself a cup of milk and ate a slice of bread.

"This house is so cosy," thought Snow White. "But it's such a mess. Whoever lives here is very untidy."

25

"I can take care of this," said Snow White to herself. "Perhaps if I make myself useful I'll be allowed to stay." Snow White found a broom and set to work. When she had finished cleaning, the girl lay down on one of the beds and fell fast asleep.

27

Late that afternoon the seven Dwarfs shouldered their tools and left the mine.

In an orderly line, according to the numbers on their hats, they filed through the forest until they reached their cottage.

"Here's to a hearty meal and a good night's rest," cried Dwarf Number One. But he stopped in surprise when he saw that the cottage door was wide open.

Alarmed, the Dwarfs peeked inside their cottage. But instead of an intruder, they saw a beautiful young girl sound asleep on one of their beds, just as if she belonged there!

"Who can this be?" the Dwarfs asked one another. But the only way to find out was to disturb their unexpected visitor. Snow White awoke with a start, then she quickly told the little men about her stepmother's wicked plot, and how she had ended up in their cottage. The Dwarfs, who were instantly won over by Snow White's gentleness and beauty, were shocked at the Queen's ruthlessness.

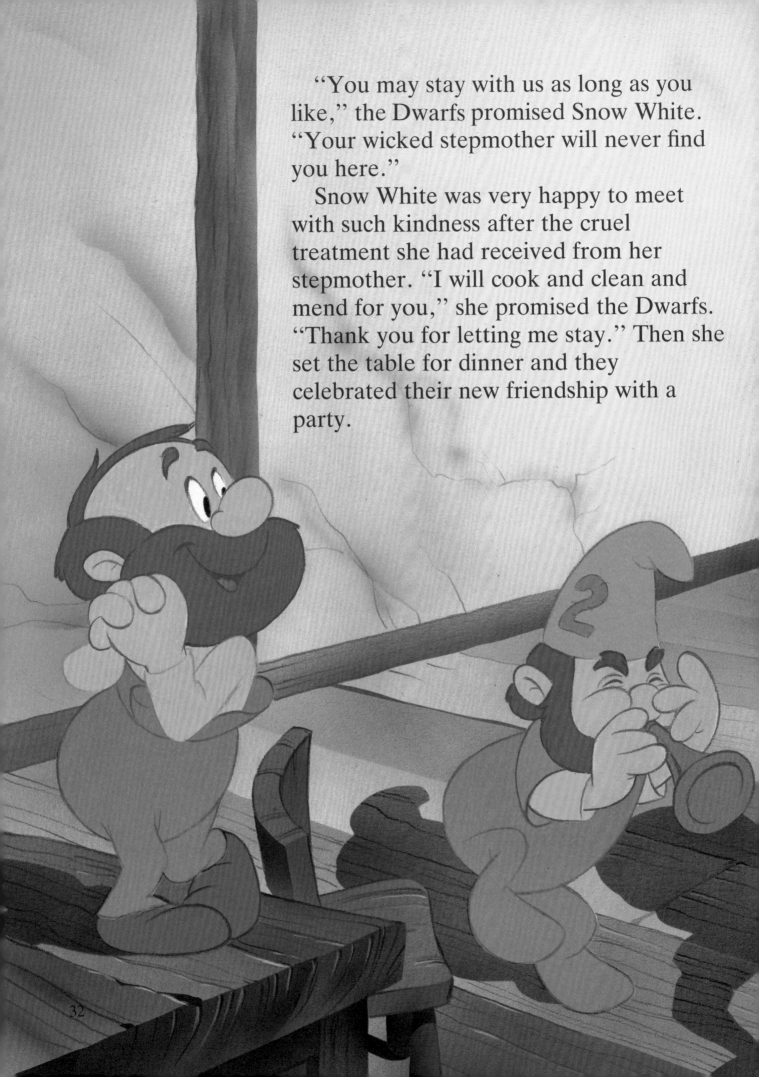

"You may stay with us as long as you like," the Dwarfs promised Snow White. "Your wicked stepmother will never find you here."

Snow White was very happy to meet with such kindness after the cruel treatment she had received from her stepmother. "I will cook and clean and mend for you," she promised the Dwarfs. "Thank you for letting me stay." Then she set the table for dinner and they celebrated their new friendship with a party.

The next morning, Snow White made a delicious breakfast of pancakes, fresh eggs, ham, and buttered toast. The Dwarfs set off for their mine well fed and in high spirits. "Now be careful of strangers," they called back to Snow White. "Don't speak to anyone you don't know."

"I won't," she answered, waving goodbye. Then, humming to herself, she went into the cottage to begin her chores.

At the castle the Queen was busy with her new plan, putting the finishing touches on her disguise. "Snow White will never recognize me as a pedlar woman!" she crowed. She stuffed her bag full of baubles and knickknacks. Then she consulted her magic book to learn the way to the Dwarfs' cottage.

The Queen walked quickly through the forest, and before long she found the little cottage in the glen. "Combs! Belts!" she called, knocking on the door. "I have the prettiest things for the best prices in the kingdom!"

Snow White opened the door a crack to peek. "I mustn't come out," she said cautiously.

"Then I'll come in," replied the Queen, pushing her way into the cottage.

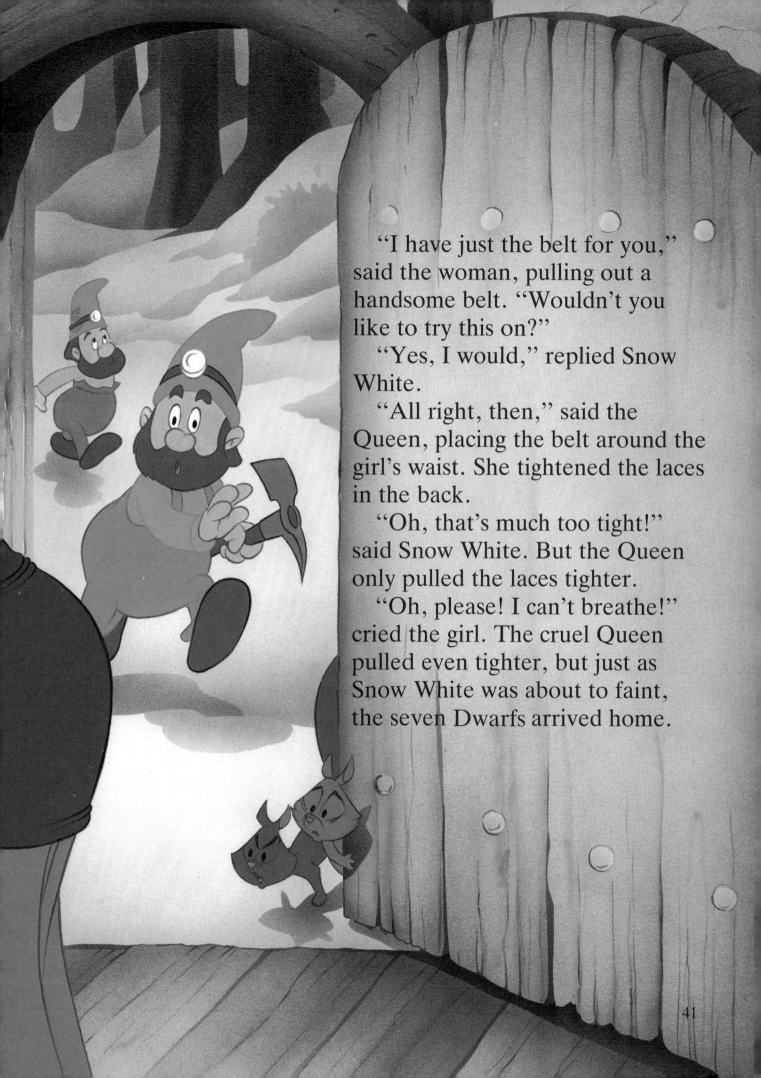

"I have just the belt for you," said the woman, pulling out a handsome belt. "Wouldn't you like to try this on?"

"Yes, I would," replied Snow White.

"All right, then," said the Queen, placing the belt around the girl's waist. She tightened the laces in the back.

"Oh, that's much too tight!" said Snow White. But the Queen only pulled the laces tighter.

"Oh, please! I can't breathe!" cried the girl. The cruel Queen pulled even tighter, but just as Snow White was about to faint, the seven Dwarfs arrived home.

The Queen fled, and some of the Dwarfs chased after her in angry pursuit. The others hurried to help Snow White, who lay shaken and gasping, on the floor. One dwarf quickly loosened the belt, while another fetched a glass of water.

"You'll be fine. You're going to be all right," soothed a third dwarf.

When the Queen returned to the castle, sure that Snow
White was dead, she asked her magic mirror again:
"Mirror, mirror, on the wall,
Who's the fairest one of all?"

44

She was enraged when the mirror replied:
"'Tis true, O Queen, that you are fair,
But Snow White's beauty's beyond compare."
    The jealous Queen flew into a fury. "I shall destroy her
yet!" she shouted at the mirror, and she devised a new
plan. Disguising herself as an old peasant woman in a
mask and ragged clothes, the Queen brewed a deadly
poison. Into it, she dipped a basketfull of apples.

The Queen made her way back to the Dwarfs' cottage. There, late in the day, she found Snow White, alone again.

"Good day, my child," she said in a feeble, trembling voice. "Would you like a ripe apple?"

The apple looked so good that Snow White forgot her trouble, and the Dwarfs' second warning against strangers. Her kindness made her unwilling to refuse the poor old woman's gift.

"Thank you," she replied. And she took a bite of the poisoned fruit.

Immediately, Snow White fell to the ground as if she were dead.

The wicked Queen laughed with pleasure. "Now I need not worry anymore," she said. "I have destroyed you myself, and I am surely the fairest in the land."

Just as the Queen turned back toward the castle, the seven Dwarfs came home and saw Snow White lying beside the spilled basket of apples.

"Who are you?" the Dwarfs demanded of the old woman. "And what have you done to our Princess?"

"Your Snow White is dead!" cried the Queen triumphantly. The angry Dwarfs raced after her with their picks, but the Queen was too fast for them, and she escaped into the forest.

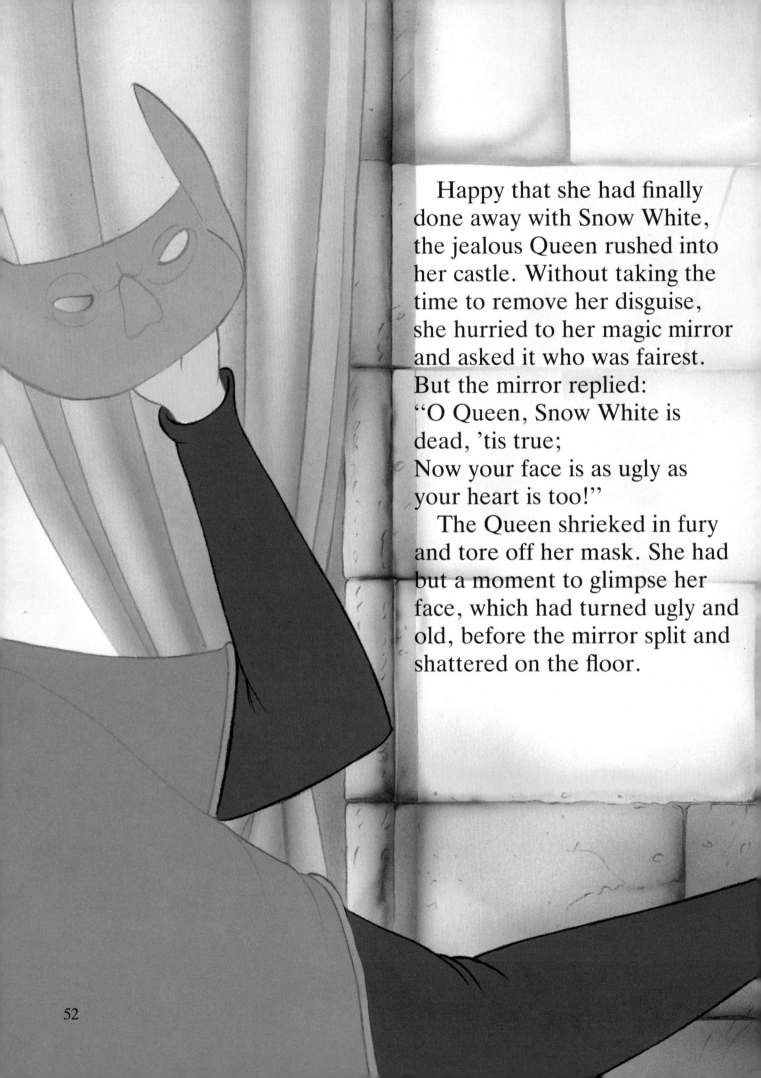

Happy that she had finally done away with Snow White, the jealous Queen rushed into her castle. Without taking the time to remove her disguise, she hurried to her magic mirror and asked it who was fairest. But the mirror replied:
"O Queen, Snow White is dead, 'tis true;
Now your face is as ugly as your heart is too!"

The Queen shrieked in fury and tore off her mask. She had but a moment to glimpse her face, which had turned ugly and old, before the mirror split and shattered on the floor.

Meanwhile, the Dwarfs had given up the chase and returned to their fallen Princess, who lay where she had fallen. The little men gathered around her lifeless body and wept. It was hard to believe that her goodness and beauty had been destroyed in a moment by her jealous stepmother.

Using their great skill as metalworkers, the Dwarfs fashioned a gleaming casket of gold and crystal. Sadly, they placed Snow White in the casket and set it atop a high hill. For many days and nights, they kept a vigil beside it.

One day, the handsome Prince of a nearby kingdom noticed the beautiful crystal-and-gold casket shining in the sun. He rode closer and saw that it contained a beautiful young woman.

The Dwarfs told him the sad story, and the Prince, too, began to weep. "For such sweet innocence to have suffered such a cruel fate," he whispered, "I feel that I love her. Let me kiss her just once before I go."

Solemnly, the Dwarfs opened the casket, and the Prince gathered Snow White in his arms. As soon as he placed a gentle kiss on her lips, Snow White opened her eyes. "Where am I?" she asked.

Love had broken the Queen's evil spell.

Overjoyed, the Prince and the Dwarfs told Snow White all that had happened since she had taken a bite of the poisoned apple. As they spoke, Snow White watched the Prince's kind face and listened to his gentle voice. The Dwarfs could see the love between them grow like magic, and shine in their eyes.

"Will you come with me to my father's castle," asked the Prince, "and be my bride?"

Snow White joyfully agreed, and bade a fond farewell to her little friends as she and the Prince rode off to his castle.

The Dwarfs were delighted that Snow White had
awakened to a new life. They danced at the wedding of their
Princess and her Prince. And the happy couple never forgot
the seven friends who had helped the Princess and brought
them together.